MY BROTHER THE CREEP

by Janet Adele Bloss

illustrated by Don Robison

Published by Willowisp Press, Inc.
401 E. Wilson Bridge Road, Worthington, Ohio 43085

Printed in the United States of America
10 9 8 7

ISBN 0-87406-030-3

To my wonderful Ohio family: Carolyn, Jack, Cheryl, Pamela, Billy, and Grandmother Frederick (the all-time, undefeated champion pie maker!)

1.

Jesse Andrews lovingly held her doll, Nicole. She looked at Nicole's little china head with her painted blue eyes and painted red lips. Nicole was a very pretty doll from France. She was Jesse's favorite out of her whole doll collection.

Jesse gazed up at the shelf on her bedroom wall. Twelve other dolls sat there, smiling. There was an empty space in the middle where Nicole usually sat.

Collecting dolls was Jesse's hobby. She'd been collecting them ever since she was nine years old. Jesse wanted to get one doll from every country in the world. So far she had a doll from Italy, Japan, Norway, Egypt, England, Scotland, Germany, Denmark, Ireland, Belgium, Switzerland, and Spain. Nicole was from France. She was the prettiest of them all in her yellow, silk dress. She had a tiny pearl necklace around her throat.

Jesse looked up as Mikey ran into the room.

"Whatcha doin'?" he asked. Mikey stood staring up at Jesse with his big brown eyes.

"Get out of my room," Jesse said. "You have to knock first. Mom said so."

"That's the dumbest doll I ever saw," Mikey said. He pointed at Nicole. "She doesn't even have socks on. And her shoes are painted. They're fake. Can I hold her?"

"No," said Jesse. "She's made out of china and you'll break her."

"No, I won't," Mikey answered.

"Yes, you will," Jesse said, annoyed.

"No, I won't," Mikey answered again.

"Yes, you will. Get out of my room," Jesse said, angrily.

What a brat, Jesse thought. Why do I have to have the worst brother in the world? Why is he always bothering me?

"You stink," Mikey said.

"I do not," Jesse sniffed. "I smell like flowers. I used bath powder. Aunt Bess and Uncle Waldo gave it to me."

The powder had been a Christmas gift. Jesse loved to use it. It made her feel very grown up. The box the powder came in was so pretty. It was shiny blue with a big, blue powder puff inside. She kept the box on the lamp stand by her bed. Sometimes in the middle of the night she would wake up, open the box, and smell the wonderful scent of roses. Then, she would go back to sleep and dream about flower gardens.

"Let me hold her," Mikey said. He pointed to Nicole again.

"No! I know you. You'll just break her or something," Jesse repeated.

Jesse thought back to all the things that Mikey had ruined. He had scribbled in her favorite horse book with a green crayon. He had put sand in her sock drawer. He had polished her white tennis shoes with mustard. The list went on and on. There was no doubt about it. He was the worst little brother in the whole world.

Jesse wondered how a little boy, only five years old, could get into so much trouble. Jesse wasn't about to let him hold a doll as fragile as Nicole. She took the French doll and carefully put her back on the shelf. There was one good thing about being the oldest kid in the house; she was the tallest. She knew that Mikey couldn't reach the shelf. So, Nicole was safe.

Mikey ran over to Jesse's bed. He climbed up on it, then started jumping as high as he could. The bed springs squeaked and the mattress shook.

"I'm flying!" Mikey screamed. "I'm flying!"

"Stop it!" yelled Jesse. She grabbed Mikey's ankle and pulled him down. "Now get out and stay out!"

"Jesse, come set the table please!" Jesse's mom called from the kitchen.

Jesse answered, "Okay, I'm coming!" She grabbed Mikey by the arm and pulled him out into the hall. "Stay out of my room," she ordered. "I mean it."

Mikey stuck his tongue out and crossed his eyes.

"I mean it," Jesse said again. She walked to the kitchen where her mother was cooking dinner. The smell of roast chicken came from the oven.

"Mom," Jesse said. "Why do I have to set the

table every night? Why can't Mikey help?"

Jesse's mom wiped her hands on her blue apron. "Oh, Jesse," she said. "We've been over this a hundred times. You know Mikey's too young to help. Why, he can't even tie his shoes, yet."

"But, I get tired of doing everything," Jesse said. "Mikey never helps."

"He's only five," Jesse's mom said. "As the oldest child, you have more responsibilities."

"But, Mom," Jesse said. "I'm only eleven. That's not so old."

"It's old enough to set the table," her mother said.

Jesse sighed. It always ended like that, she thought. She always lost. She always had to give in. And what about Mikey? Dumb old Mikey never had to do anything. Dumb old Mikey always got his way because he was younger.

Jesse put plates on the dining room table: one for herself, one for Dad, one for Mom, and one for Mikey, Mikey the monster. When she placed the glasses on the table, everyone, except Mikey, got one. He didn't get a glass. He got a special clown cup. Uncle Waldo and Aunt Bess had brought it to him from Disney World. At the bottom of the cup was a clown's face with a bright red nose. After

Mikey drank all of his milk, he could see the face on the bottom. He would laugh when he saw the clown's face smiling back at him. But, he would cry if he didn't get his special cup. So, Jesse put it by Mikey's plate every night. But this night she first stared into the cup and frowned back at the clown's smiling face.

After Jesse finished setting the table, she walked back to her bedroom. She noticed that the door was closed.

That's funny, she thought. I don't remember closing it. Oh, no! That means Mikey's in there!

Jesse ran to her room and threw the door open.

"Look at me!" Mikey yelled. He laughed as he stood in the middle of Jesse's room. He was covered from head to toe with white powder. It was Jesse's special bath powder. Mikey looked like a little snow-boy. His hair wasn't brown anymore. It was white. Even his shoes were white.

"I don't stink either," yelled Mikey. "I smell like flowers. Lots of flowers!"

"What are you doing?" Jesse shouted. "Mother, come quick!" Jesse tried to grab Mikey, but he ran by her, leaving little white footprints on the floor.

"What's wrong?" her mother asked. She rushed into Jesse's room.

10

"Look!" Jesse wailed. She pointed at the shiny, blue box lying empty on the floor and the circle of white powder around it. "Look what Mikey did!"

"What a mess," her mother said. "Mikey! Mikey, come here!" she called.

Jesse and her mom waited. Finally, a little head peered around the doorway. It was a chalk-white head with powdery hair. Mikey's big brown eyes looked scared. "What?" he asked in a tiny voice.

"Young man, did you make this mess?" his mother asked. "Did you get into your sister's bath powder?"

"She told me I could," Mikey said.

"I did not!" Jesse shouted. "I never said that! You little liar!"

"Jesse! Don't call your brother a liar," her mother said.

Jesse thought to herself, Why can't I call him a liar? He's lying, isn't he? So, that makes him a liar! I could call him something worse.

"Young man, you've been told to stay out of your sister's room. You'll have to be punished." Jesse's mom looked very serious. "Come here, please."

Mikey hung his head. His eyes filled with tears. He walked to his mother.

"One swat will do it," his mother said. She slapped her hand lightly against Mikey's bottom. A cloud of powder puffed out at her. "Achoo!" she sneezed.

"Achoo! Achoo!" Jesse sneezed, too.

Mikey cried. Tears fell onto his powdery T-shirt.

"You baby! That didn't hurt," Jesse said. "Mom barely touched you." She turned to her mother and asked, "Can I spank him, Mom? He was in my room. So, I should spank him, too."

"No," Jesse's mother said. "He's been punished enough. Let's clean up this mess and get dinner on the table. I just heard your father pull into the driveway."

"Daddy's home! Daddy's home!" Jesse and Mikey both shouted. Mikey had completely forgotten his tears. Jesse wondered if maybe she was too old for shouting. But, she couldn't stop. She was excited that Daddy was home.

Jesse and Mikey ran to the living room. In walked Daddy. He seemed so tall to Jesse. She looked up at him and held her arms out. He leaned down and gave her a hug. "There's my big girl," he said, giving her a quick kiss on the forehead. Then, he held Mikey under the arms. He tossed Mikey high into the air and caught him. A cloud of powder puffed into the air.

"Whew! What's this? Did Winkypopper fall into a flour barrel?" Jesse's dad asked. Winkypopper was his pet name for Mikey.

"No, I fell in Jesse's powder," Mikey said.

"He did not!" Jesse frowned. "He got into my special bath powder and spilled it all. But, Mom spanked him." Jesse smiled at the memory.

"Hm-m-m," her dad said. "It sounds like Stardoodle's had a rough day." Jesse's dad sometimes

13

called her Stardoodle. It didn't really make any sense. But, Jesse liked it. It was her special name.

"Dinner will be ready in ten minutes," Jesse's mother said. "The rolls are almost done."

"Great," her dad said. "That gives me time to show Mikey what I got for him on the way home. Here you go, son." He handed Mikey a shoe box with holes in the lid.

"What is it?" Mikey asked. His dad grinned. Mikey took the lid off and looked inside. "Oh, boy!" he shouted.

Jesse looked into the box and said, "Oh, no! P.U." She held her nose.

Her mother looked in the box and said, "Oh, Gary! Don't you think Mikey's too young?"

"Too young for a frog?" Jesse's dad said. "I had a frog when I was his age. Every boy should have his own frog."

"Oh, boy!" Mikey said again. Mikey lifted the frog out and held it in his hands. It stared back at him with bulging eyes. The frog's skin was spotted and brown and baggy. Its white throat moved as its heart beat.

"That's gross!" Jesse said. "Keep it away from me. Frogs give you warts. When you hold them you get covered with bumps."

"Now, Jesse," her dad said. "That's just an old wive's tale. There's no truth to it. Frogs never gave anyone bumps."

"That's his name," Mikey said. "Mr. Bump. My frog's name is Mr. Bump and anyone who touches him will get bumps. Anyone, but me."

"I wouldn't want to touch your old frog, anyway," Jesse said.

"Where in the world did you find him?" Jesse's mother asked. She looked at her husband with a curious smile.

"By Old Man Camber's Woods," Jesse's dad replied. "He was sitting in the road, so I stopped the car. His home must be in the woods. Maybe he got lost. I don't know. Anyway, I picked him up. I was going to put him back in the woods, but I thought Mikey might like to have him." He winked at Mikey.

Jesse listened. She knew about Old Man Camber's Woods. Some of the kids said the woods were haunted. The woods weren't too far away and sometimes she had to walk by them. But, Jesse never really walked by the woods. She *ran* by them. Some of the kids said that Old Man Camber's ghost still lived in the woods. But, Jesse didn't like to think about that. My dad must be pretty brave to stop by the woods, she thought. But then, her dad didn't believe in ghosts.

"Put Mr. Bump in your room for now," her mother said to Mikey. "Make sure the lid's on tight. And wash your hands! It's time for dinner."

"Me and Mr. Bump's gonna go wash our hands," Mikey said. "Mr. Bump's my best friend."

Jesse thought to herself, They make a pretty good pair, my brother and a frog.

Jesse's mother looked at her husband. "Oh, Gary," she said. "I don't know if this house is big enough for all of us and a frog, too. I just hope Mr. Bump behaves himself." She looked at Jesse. "Honey, would you make sure Mikey washes his hands? I don't want him coming to the table smelling like Mr. Bump."

"Mr. *Yuk*," Jesse said. She walked back to the bathroom and watched Mikey wash his hands.

"Can Mr. Bump sit on the shelf with your dolls?" Mikey asked.

"No," said Jesse.

"Why not?" Mikey asked.

"Because he's slimy and he smells," she said. Jesse thought about how dumb a five-year-old brother could be. She wondered if she might go crazy living with him. Could his dumbness rub off? Jesse hoped not.

"Hurry up," she said. "It's time for dinner."

"Can Mr. Bump drink out of my clown cup?" Mikey asked.

"No," Jesse said.

"Why not?" Mikey looked at Jesse with wondering eyes.

Jesse didn't say anything. She rolled her eyes and thought, What a dumb question! How can one person ask so many dumb questions? He's driving me nuts!

2.

The next morning Jesse sat at the breakfast table. Her mother set a plate of poached eggs and toast before her.

"Pass the salt, please," Jesse said.

"Don't use too much," her father warned as he passed it. "A lot of salt isn't good for you."

Jesse's dad was kind of a health nut. She tried to go along with it and taste some of the things he said were good. One time she even tried something called *tofu*. It tasted like rotten cottage cheese. After the tofu, Jesse stuck to safer things, like bean sprouts and granola. Jesse tried to get her dad to eat an occasional cupcake or candy bar, but he said he'd rather eat laundry soap. Jesse thought that was a strange thing to say.

"Mr. Bump can eat all the salt he wants," Mikey informed them. "Mr. Bump loves salt." Mikey pounded his spoon against the breakfast table.

"That's the most stupid thing I've ever heard," Jesse said. "Frogs don't eat salt. They eat bugs and stuff like that."

"Now, Jesse. Don't call your brother stupid," her mother said. "Mikey, you must never, never give Mr. Bump salt to eat. That would make him sick. We'll give him water. And we'll catch some bugs for him, too. Today, we'll make a nice cage for him. You can even let him hop around in the yard, okay?"

"He can't," Mikey said. "Mr. Bump is going to school."

"What?" Jesse's father set his glass of mango juice on the table and looked at Mikey. "What did you say?"

"Mr. Bump is going to school with Jesse," Mikey said again.

"No way," said Jesse. "I wouldn't be caught dead with that fat frog hopping along with me."

"No one will see him," Mikey said. "He'll hide in your lunch box."

Jesse sat quietly for a minute. She looked at her lunch box on the table beside her plate. She opened the latch and very slowly lifted the lid, just a crack.

Jesse stared through the crack and saw two little bulging eyes staring back at her. She closed the lid quickly. "Oh, gross!" she yelled. "There's a frog in my lunch box, yuk! Dad, make Mikey take that thing out of my lunch box."

"Let me see that," her dad said. Before Jesse

could say another word, her father took the lunch box and opened the lid.

A big green and brown frog sat inside, looking out with froggy eyes. "Ribbit," Mr. Bump croaked.

"Mikey! Frogs do not belong in lunch boxes," his mom said. "Put Mr. Bump back in his own box." She reached into the lunch box and picked up Mr. Bump. He tried to jump away, but she held him.

"I can't carry my lunch in that smelly old thing,"

Jesse complained. "Frog juice will get on my sandwich!"

"Don't worry," said her mom. "Your sandwich is still in the refrigerator. You can take your lunch in a paper bag today. I'll clean out your lunch box with hot water and soap."

"Oh, yuk! I'll never use that lunch box again," Jesse said. She glared at Mikey.

Jesse's father spoke in his low voice. It was the heavy voice he used when he was angry. Even though he wasn't angry at her, it still made Jesse kind of nervous to hear it.

"Young man," he said. "I want you to put that frog in his own box. Don't you ever put him in your sister's lunch box again. Do you understand me?"

"Yes," Mikey said. His voice was squeaky. Jesse could tell he was trying not to cry.

"Aren't you going to spank him?" Jesse asked. Her father looked at her with a frown that made her wish she hadn't asked.

Just then, they heard a knock at the kitchen door.

"Come in," Jesse's mother called. The door opened and in walked two little girls. They each carried a lunch box in one hand and books under the other arm.

"Good morning, Biff," Jesse's mother said to the

one with her hair in braids.

"Good morning, Karen," her mother said to the shorter one with freckles. "How's your little sister? Is Kimmy feeling better?"

"Good morning, Mrs. Andrews," Karen said. "Yeah, Kimmy's better today. But, she still has to stay in bed. Mom says it was just the flu. But, Kimmy still needs rest."

"Well, I'm glad to hear Kimmy's better." Jesse's mother turned to look at her. "Are you done, Jesse?" she asked. "Finish your juice."

Jesse gulped it down. It was papaya juice that her father said was good. It tasted okay. In fact, she kind of liked it. Anything was better than tofu.

Jesse jumped up from the table. "Let's go!" she said.

"Would you girls like a lift?" Jesse's dad asked. "I'm leaving for work now. I'd be glad to drop you off."

"No thanks, Dad," Jesse said. She looked at Karen and Biff. "Let's walk, okay? We've got time."

Karen and Biff nodded. "Bye," they said. The three girls walked out into the yard.

"Have a nice day," Jesse's mother called. "Study hard."

The girls waved goodbye. They walked down the

sidewalk toward school. The three girls walked the twenty minutes to school together almost every morning. Sometimes in the winter when it snowed, they got a ride with Jesse's dad.

But today, the sun was out and the sky was blue. Birds sang from the trees. It was the beginning of spring.

"What kind of sandwich do you have today?" Biff asked Jesse.

"Peanut butter and jelly," Jesse said.

"Ick, don't you ever get tired of that?" Karen asked.

"Nope, I could eat a million of them," Jesse said, rubbing her stomach.

"I'll bet you couldn't," Biff added.

"Well, maybe just a thousand," Jesse smiled.

They laughed. Jesse, Karen, and Biff laughed the way that best friends laugh at silliness, at nothing, and at peanut butter and jelly sandwiches.

"Let's do something fun," Karen said.

"Like what?" Jesse asked.

"Oh, I don't know." Karen scratched her ear.

"I've got an idea. Let's go roller skating after school today," Jesse suggested. "We can skate on the playground."

"I can't," Karen said. "I have to go straight home.

Kimmy's sick. Mom needs me to stay with her while she goes to the store." Karen sighed. "Little sisters can be such a pain," she said.

"They can't be half as bad as little brothers," Jesse said. "Nobody's as bad as my little brother."

"I'll bet Kimmy is. She cries all the time and she always gets her way. I have to do everything for her. She's such a baby," Karen complained.

"If you think that's bad, then you don't know Mikey," Jesse said. "He colors in my books. He messes up my dolls' hair. He never flushes the toilet. He's really gross."

"Boy, are you lucky," Karen said. She looked at Biff. "It must be nice not to have any brothers or sisters. I'll bet you get twice as much for Christmas."

"It's okay," Biff said. "Sometimes it gets lonely. I'm alone a lot."

"You can borrow Mikey anytime you want," Jesse laughed.

"Yeah, if you ever feel lonely just give me a call," Karen said. "I'll bring Kimmy right over."

"Look at that cloud," Biff said. She pointed up at the sky. "Doesn't it look like Mrs. Knot-head?"

The girls giggled. Mrs. Nother was the fifth grade gym teacher. But some of the kids called her Mrs. Knot-head.

"It kind of looks like Mrs. Knot-head," Jesse said. "But, the cloud shape has wheels instead of legs. The wind is blowing her across the sky."

Jesse, Karen, and Biff turned a corner and crossed the street. Karen and Biff swung their lunch boxes by their sides.

"So, what are we going to do?" Karen asked. "I can't do anything after school, because of Kimmy. Let's do something this weekend."

"I've got it!" Jesse cried out. "I'll have a slumber party this Saturday. You two come over and bring your sleeping bags. Mom will let us sleep in the family room. I know she will. We can make ice cream floats, okay?"

"Yeah!" the girls shouted. "That sounds great!"

The three friends stopped to shake hands. Then, they walked on.

Suddenly, from out of nowhere came a growling sound. The girls stopped and listened. The sound came closer.

"There it is!" Biff shouted. She pointed at a tree beside the sidewalk. Behind the tree was a big dog. It was furry and gray. Its long yellow teeth showed in a terrible snarl. It seemed to be ready to jump out at them.

"G-r-r-r," the dog snarled. "Gr-r-r-r-r-r."

"Come on," Karen said quietly. "Let's slowly walk away." She turned to Jesse and said in a whisper, "Walk very slowly, Jesse. Come on."

Karen and Biff began to take short, slow steps. But, Jesse stood still. She stood and stared at the dog. "I can't," she said. "I can't move."

"She's too scared to move," Biff said to Karen. "We have to do something. The dog's getting closer."

The dog snapped its teeth together. It crawled forward inch by inch toward Jesse's feet. She stood and stared. She couldn't move. Her arms hung at her sides.

The dog laid its ears flat against its head. It was ready to jump.

"Now!" yelled Karen. As she shouted, she pulled Jesse out of the way. At the same time Biff jumped forward. She smacked the dog's nose with her lunch box.

The dog yelped and howled. Then, it tucked its tail between its legs. The dog turned around and quickly crawled back behind the tree. It peeped out at them from behind the trunk. The dog growled very quietly now. But, it stayed behind the tree.

Karen and Biff took Jesse's arms. They led her down the sidewalk between them.

"It's a good thing we were with you," Karen said.

"Yeah," said Biff. "You know, Jesse, you've got to learn not to be so afraid of dogs. I've never known anyone as afraid of dogs as you. It's a good thing we were together."

"It sure was," said Jesse. "Thanks."

3.

On the following Saturday, Jesse welcomed Biff and Karen to the slumber party.

"Put your sleeping bags over here," Jesse said. "Let's put them under the window. That way we can look out and see the stars. We can pretend we're outside."

Karen and Biff both said, "Okay." They carried their sleeping bags over to the window and put them on the floor.

Mikey ran into the room. "Old MacDonald had a farm, ee-i-ee-i-o," he sang at the top of his lungs.

Karen and Biff looked at each other and giggled.

"Go away, Creep!" Jesse said sternly.

"With a quack-quack here," sang Mikey.

"I mean it," said Jesse. "Get lost!"

"And a moo-moo there." Mikey's song was more like shouting than singing. Finally, the words gave way completely to animal noises. "Oink! Oink!" Mikey shrieked.

Jesse felt her anger rising. He's driving me nuts,

she thought. He's ruining my slumber party. He ruins everything!

Jesse jumped up and chased Mikey around the room. "Stop it!" she yelled.

"Oink-oink-quack-quack-moo-moo!" Mikey shouted as he ran. He darted out the doorway, down the hall and to his bedroom. Jesse heard him slam the door.

Jesse breathed quickly from running after Mikey. She looked at Karen and Biff and said, "I'm sorry, you guys. That's my brother, the creep. He's such a pest. I'd sell the creep if I knew anyone dumb enough to buy him." Jesse tried to smile.

"It's okay," said Karen. "I know what it's like."

"No, you don't," said Jesse. "*Nobody's* as bad as Mikey. Nobody else finds a frog in their lunch box or mustard on their shoes or sand in their socks. He even dumped my bath powder on the floor." Jesse scratched her head. "What I can't figure out is, how can Mom and Dad stand him? If I was them I'd give him away."

"We can have the next slumber party at my house," Biff said. "Nobody will bother us there." She looked at her watch. "Hey!" she said. "It's getting late."

* * * * * *

"Look at these slippers," Karen said. "Aren't they wild?" She showed her slippers to Jesse and Biff. They were gray and fuzzy. The part over the toes looked like an elephant's head. A little trunk curled up. Pink floppy ears stuck out on the side.

"Those are neat," Jesse said. "Where'd you get them?"

"Mom got them for me," Karen laughed.

"Where's its other eye?" Biff asked. "Your left slipper only has one eye."

Karen frowned. She looked closely at her slipper. "Oh, that," she said. "Kimmy tore the eye off. Nothing's safe around her."

"Let's go into my room and change into our pajamas," Jesse said. "Then, after we talk some more, we can make ice cream floats."

"Yea!" squealed Biff. "Ice cream. You scream. We all scream for ice cream! Yea!"

"What flavors do you have?" Karen asked.

"Mom got blueberry and Rocky Road," Jesse said.

"M-m-m-m. I love blueberry," said Biff, as she licked her lips. "I'm glad you didn't buy the ice cream."

"Why?" Jesse asked.

"Because you would have gotten peanut butter

and jelly!" Biff smiled and Jesse and Karen giggled.

The three girls went to Jesse's bedroom. They changed into their pajamas. Biff wore an old shirt of her father's that came to her knees. She rolled the sleeves up.

Karen wore blue pajamas with yellow daisies on the front. She put the elephant slippers on her feet.

Jesse changed into her tan-colored pajamas. She pulled the top over her head. On the front was a picture of a horse.

Afterward, the girls walked back to the family room. They sat on the floor and began talking.

"Look how long my bangs are getting," Biff said. "My father says I look like a shaggy dog."

"Dogs! Br-r-r," Jesse shivered. "Don't say that word around me."

"Look! What's that?" Karen gasped. "Look! Something's moving over there." She pointed her finger at the sleeping bags. One of the sleeping bags had a big lump in it. The lump wiggled and moved.

"All right," Jesse said. "Come on out of there, right now. Mikey, I know it's you. Come out. I mean it."

"No." Mikey's voice was muffled from inside the bag.

"Come out right now!" Jesse demanded.

31

"No!" Mikey giggled. "You can't make me," he said.

"See what a creep he is," Jesse said to Biff and Karen.

"You can't make me come out," Mikey repeated.

"Yes, I can." Jesse ran over to the sleeping bag. She sat on the squirming lump.

"Ow!" Mikey shouted. "Ow! You're hurting me. You're on my hand. Ow! You're on my head. Get off!"

"Will you come out?" Jesse asked. She smiled at Biff and Karen. They both giggled. It was quite a sight. Jesse sat on the yelling, wiggling lump. She looked like a rodeo rider.

"Yes! Yes! I'll come out," Mikey said. "Get off!"

Jesse stood up. Mikey crawled out of the sleeping bag. His hair was a mess. He rubbed his ear. "You hurt me," he said.

"Serves you right," said Jesse. "You shouldn't be in other peoples' sleeping bags."

"You're mean," Mikey said.

"You're dumb," Jesse said. "Now, go away. We're making ice cream floats."

"Can I help?" Mikey asked.

"No, go away." Jesse said loudly.

"Please? I promise I'll be good," Mikey pleaded.

Jesse glared at her brother. Mikey got a stubborn look on his face.

"I won't go away," he said. "I'm going to sit right here." Mikey plopped himself down in the middle of the room.

"Mom!" Jesse called. "Mom!"

Jesse's mother came into the room. "Yes, what is it?" she said.

"Make Mikey go away," Jesse pleaded. "He's just sitting there, and he's bothering us. He won't leave us alone. Please, make him go away."

Jesse's mother looked at Mikey sitting cross-legged on the floor. "Just walk around him, dear," she said to Jesse. "He's not bothering anything."

"But, Mom!" Jesse pleaded.

"Just walk around him. He'll get tired soon enough. Then he'll go away," her mother said, as she left the room.

"You big baby," Jesse whispered at Mikey.

"Ha-ha-ha. Mommy said I could stay," Mikey said. He sat on the floor and watched the girls.

Jesse, Karen, and Biff sat down on the floor at the other end of the room.

"What should we do?" Biff whispered.

"Let's go make the ice cream floats, now," Karen said.

"No," Jesse said. "He'll just follow us. We have to get rid of Mikey first. He'll spy on us all night if we don't." She closed her eyes for a minute and thought. "I've got it!" she said, opening her eyes. "Let's tell ghost stories."

"What?" Karen said. "That's a crazy idea."

Biff smiled. "Oh, I see what you mean," she said. She whispered to Karen, "We'll scare Mikey."

"Oh, yeah," Karen said. "Okay, you start," she said, looking at Jesse.

34

Jesse reached up onto the table. She turned off the lamp. The room was dark. Mikey, listening, sat in the middle of the room. Jesse leaned forward and spoke in a very low, quiet voice.

"Once upon a time," Jesse said, "there was a little boy. He had big brown eyes and brown hair. He was five years old. Sometimes he forgot to flush the toilet."

"Yuk," Biff said.

"Sh-sh-sh!" said Karen.

Jesse began to talk again. "Well, this little boy sometimes didn't know when to leave. One day he was in the house of an old, old lady. This lady had green hair and a big nose and sharp teeth. She had spiders all over her. Her hands were skeleton hands. This lady was a bad old witch, but the little boy didn't know it."

Biff made soft ghost noises. She sang, "Oo-ooooo-ooooo!" in a very high voice.

Mikey's eyes opened wider. He put his thumb in his mouth.

"This little boy wouldn't leave," Jesse said. "The mean old witch got very angry. So do you know what she did?"

"What?" asked Biff.

"What?" asked Karen.

"Wh-wh-what?" whispered Mikey.

"This old lady decided to make the little boy into ice cream," Jesse said. "Shivery, cold, freezing ice cream."

Karen giggled. "Sh-sh-sh!" Biff warned.

"Ice cream?" Mikey whispered.

"Yes, ice cream," Jesse said. "This old lady witch could turn anyone into ice cream. Then she would eat him up." Jesse said the words 'eat him up' very softly.

"So, the mean old witch took the little boy. She put him in a big bowl. She cracked eggs on his head. She stirred him up with a big spoon. The boy yelled and yelled. He yelled his head off. But no one would come to help him. No one would come to help the little boy," Jesse said with a very scary voice.

"Why?" whispered Biff.

"Why?" asked Karen.

"Wh-wh-why?" asked Mikey.

"Because," Jesse said, "this little boy didn't know when to leave. That's why nobody would help him. So, the mean old witch with green hair made him into ice cream. The ice cream smelled bad. It was purple. It was the purplest ice cream in the world. The witch got a spoon and put some ice cream on it. She opened her mouth. She put the purple, little boy ice cream in her mouth. She chewed it up with her sharp teeth and . . ."

"Mommy! Daddy! Jesse's scaring me!" Mikey jumped up. He ran from the room. He yelled, "Mommy! Daddy! Mommy!"

Jesse, Karen, and Biff rolled on the floor. They laughed and laughed.

"Did you see his eyes?" Jesse asked. "Boy, was he scared!"

"Did you see how fast he jumped up?" Biff giggled.

"Did you see him when you reached the part about spiders all over her?" Karen asked, laughing.

The three girls sat up when they heard footsteps coming down the hall. Jesse's mother walked in.

"Jesse, why did you scare your brother?" her mother asked.

"Because he wouldn't leave," Jesse said. "He was bothering us."

"Oh, Jesse," her mother shook her head. "He's only five years old. He doesn't know any better."

"He's a pest," Jesse said. "He wouldn't leave us alone."

"Well, Daddy's in with him now trying to get him to sleep. Mikey thinks there's a witch under his bed. Oh, Jesse," her mother said. "You really shouldn't have scared him like that. Now, you girls go ahead and make your floats and don't make a mess. I'll see you in the morning. Goodnight."

"Goodnight, Mom," Jesse said.

"Goodnight, Mrs. Andrews," Biff and Karen said.

Jesse's mother left the room.

"At last!" Jesse said. "Let's make some ice cream floats! Come on!"

All three of them ran to the kitchen. Karen got glasses down from the cabinet. Biff took three long spoons from the drawer. Jesse took two cartons of ice cream from the freezer. She opened each one. "M-m-m-m," she said. "I love ice cream. What flavor does everyone want?" she asked.

Biff and Karen looked carefully at the ice cream.

"Rocky Road," said Biff.

"Rocky Road," said Karen.

"What's the matter? I thought you guys liked blueberry?" Jesse asked. "What's wrong with it?"

"It's purple," Karen said. She and Biff wrinkled their noses. "It looks like that ice cream the witch made, that smelly little boy ice cream."

Jesse looked at the purple ice cream. "Yuk," she said. "I think I'll have Rocky Road, too."

4.

"Mom, do we have any potato chips? Do we have any lemonade? Does my hair look dumb this way? Should I take the ribbon out?" Jesse asked.

"Jesse, Jesse. Calm down," her mother said. "Why are you so nervous?"

Jesse stopped walking around the room. She looked up at her mother. "Jim Huston is coming over," she said. "He's going to help me with my arithmetic homework." Jesse emptied her pants pockets. She threw gum wrappers and fuzz balls into the trash.

Her mother smiled. "Jim Huston?" she asked. "Isn't he in the sixth grade?"

"Yeah," Jesse said. "He's a year older and knows all the fifth grade arithmetic. He's going to help me with long division."

"That's nice," her mother said. "Are you having problems with your homework?"

"Just a few problems. I can do it with a little help, though. Does my hair look okay? Mikey said my hair looks like a mop. It doesn't, does it?"

"No, dear," her mother said. "Your hair looks very nice. Mikey's just teasing you." Her mother took a paper bag from the kitchen cabinet. "Here are some potato chips," she said. "I'll put them in a bowl for you. I'll make some lemonade, too. You go on and get ready."

"Thanks, Mom." Jesse ran from the kitchen. She began to clean the living room. Newspapers were on the floor. A pillow had fallen behind the couch.

"What are you doing?" Mikey asked. He walked into the room with his hands in his pockets.

"I'm cleaning up," Jesse said. "I have a friend coming over. Please stay in your room and don't bother us, okay?"

"Me and Mr. Bump are going to the moon," Mikey said. "We're flying there in a big rocket."

"Good," said Jesse. "I hope you and Mr. Bump stay there forever."

"Me and Mr. Bump know how to talk moon talk," Mikey said. "Nobody can talk moon talk, but us."

"Good. Why don't you and Mr. Bump get ready for your trip?" Jesse suggested. "You'd better go so the rocket won't leave without you."

"Okay," Mikey said. "We better get ready." He left the family room.

Great, Jesse thought to herself. For once, my little brother is going to keep busy.

She went out to the kitchen. Her mother was just opening the kitchen door. "I'll be in the backyard," she said. "I've got to weed the garden." She pulled on her gardening gloves. "The chips are on the counter. Say hello to Jim for me. Have a nice study session."

"Thanks. I will," Jesse said.

Her mother stepped out into the backyard. Jesse walked into the living room just in time to hear a knock at the front door. She quickly bent over and tied her shoe lace. Then, she opened the door.

"Hi, Jim," she said.

"Hi, Jesse." Jim was a few inches taller than Jesse. He had curly red hair. His ears stuck out just a little. Jesse thought he was cute.

"Come on in," Jesse said. She opened the door wider.

Jim walked into the living room. Jesse saw he was wearing a jacket with a picture of a tiger on the back of it.

"Have a seat," Jesse said, motioning toward the family room. "Want some lemonade?"

41

"Sure." Jim walked into the family room.

Jesse went into the kitchen. She returned, carrying a pitcher of lemonade, two glasses and a bowl of potato chips on a tray. She placed the tray on the table where Jim had put his books.

"Thanks," Jim said. He drank some lemonade. "M-mmm, that's good."

"Thank you," Jesse said. She sat in the chair beside Jim and took a sip from her glass. "How do you like sixth grade?" she asked. "Is it a lot harder than fifth?"

Jim scratched his chin and thought about it for a minute. "I guess it's harder," he said. "But, it doesn't really seem that much harder. I mean, I've always been pretty good at arithmetic and stuff like that." He looked at Jesse. "What do you like in school?" he asked. "I already know you don't like arithmetic that much," he laughed.

Jesse laughed, too. "I'm not bad at arithmetic," she said. "I'm just not good at it, either. I guess I like reading the best. And spelling."

Jesse looked shyly at Jim. "Should we get down to work?" she asked.

"Yeah," Jim said. "Just tell me what I can help you with."

"Well," Jesse said, "what I'm having trouble with

is long division." She opened her arithmetic book. "Like this one here. What I can't understand is . . ."

The soft sound of a mumbling voice came out of the air. It said, "Bibby-gibby-rivvety-pop."

Jim looked up from his book. "What was that?" he asked.

"Nothing," Jesse said. "It was nothing."

"I thought I heard something," Jim said. "It must have been my imagination."

"Yeah," Jesse said. She pointed back at the book. "Now, here's a hard one. It says 796 into 34,512. How do you get 7 into 3?"

"Well, first of all," Jim said, "you have to . . ."

"Scrubby-dubby-pippity-pop." The voice came again.

"I know I heard something that time," Jim said. He brushed his red hair from his eyes. He looked around the room. "Who's that?" he asked. He pointed to a head sticking up from behind the couch.

There was Mikey. He had squeezed himself between the couch and the wall. His head looked like a little beach ball with eyes. Mikey stared back at Jim. "Lop-pop-rickety-sop," he said.

Jim turned to Jesse. "What's he saying? Who is that?" he asked.

"That's my little brother," Jesse said. She was so embarrassed. She didn't want to yell at Mikey in front of Jim. She couldn't throw a pillow at Mikey's head, not now anyway. Although, that's what she felt like doing.

"Birken-firken-quack," Mikey said. He rolled his eyes around.

"What's wrong with him?" Jim asked. "Can't he talk?"

"He thinks he's on the moon. He said he was going on a rocket ship with Mr. Bump to the moon. He thinks he's talking moon talk. He says only he and Mr. Bump can talk moon talk."

"Who's Mr. Bump?" Jim asked.

"A frog." Jesse couldn't believe it. Why did Mikey ruin everything? Everything! Now, Jim would think she came from a weird family. He would think she was weird, too.

"What's it like on the moon?" Jim asked Mikey.

Mikey climbed up over top of the couch. He fell onto the cushions. "It smells like frogs," he said. "And everyone has red hair."

"Mikey! You stop that," Jesse said. She couldn't be quiet any longer. She just had to get Mikey out of the room. "I'm sorry," she said to Jim. "He's only five. He's a real pest."

44

"Am not," Mikey said. "I'm a real moon man. And so is Mr. Bump."

Mikey reached under the couch. He pulled out a big greenish-brown frog. "See?" he said. "Mr. Bump was on the moon. That's why he smells like a frog." Mikey carried Mr. Bump over to the table where Jesse and Jim were working.

"Get that thing away from here," Jesse said. "Put him back in his box, right now!" Jesse looked at Jim. He just sat there staring at Mikey. Oh, Jim will never come back, Jesse thought. He'll never help me with my homework again. He'll think we're all crazy.

Mikey put Mr. Bump on the table. The frog looked at Jim with big, bulging eyes. "Ribbit," it said. And then the frog jumped. It jumped right onto Jim's arithmetic book. It jumped again knocking over Jim's glass of lemonade. The glass fell over with a crash. The lemonade splattered on the books and papers . . . and on Jim.

Jim jumped away from the table. "Mikey!" Jesse yelled. She grabbed Mikey and spanked him on the bottom. Mikey began to cry. Mr. Bump sat in the spreading pool of lemonade on the table.

Everything was ruined. It was awful. It was terrible. Jesse didn't know what to do.

"I'd better go now," Jim said. He held his book up. Lemonade ran out of the pages and dripped onto the table.

"Oh, I'm so sorry," Jesse said. "I'm sorry about your book and your pants. I'm sorry about everything. I'm . . ."

"It's okay," Jim said. "I'd better go home and get cleaned up. This stuff is sticky." Jim put his book under his arm. "Is it always like this around here?" he asked.

"Only when Mikey's around," Jesse said. She felt like crying. Mikey ruined everything, she thought to herself. Jim is leaving. He'll probably never come back.

"Bye," Jim said. He closed the front door.

Jesse stood looking at the mess on the table. Her homework was soaked in lemonade. So were the potato chips. A big, brown frog sat in the middle of all of it. Mikey, crying, stood by the table.

Just then Jesse's mother walked into the room. "What's going on here?" she asked. "Where's Jim? Mikey, what's wrong, honey?"

"Oh, Mom. It was awful," Jesse said. She held back the tears.

"Jesse hit me! Jesse hit me!" Mikey wailed. He ran to his mother and hugged her legs. He sobbed.

Jesse told her mother the whole story: how Mikey talked like a moon man . . . how he said people on the moon had red hair . . . how he put Mr. Bump on the table . . . and how Mr. Bump knocked the lemonade over. "Oh, Mother. Jim will never come here again," Jesse said. "And it's all because of Mikey. That brat."

"Jesse," her mother said. "I'm sorry about what happened. But honey, remember Mikey's only five years old. He doesn't mean to be bad. He just doesn't understand, yet."

Oh no, Jesse thought to herself. It's the same old thing. Mikey gets away with it again. He does anything he wants to. And I have to understand because I'm the oldest. I have to put up with it just because he's younger. It's not fair. It's just not fair.

"I'll help you clean up this mess," her mother said. "Then, would you set the dining room table, please? Your father will be home soon." She patted Mikey's head. He stopped crying and quietly stood beside her. Then he lifted Mr. Bump off the table and held him.

Jesse felt terrible. She felt like a balloon ready to pop. She went to the kitchen and took the dinner dishes from the cabinet. On the shelf was Mikey's clown cup. Jesse took it down and looked inside. There was that dumb old clown face smiling back. "Dumb old clown. Dumb old Mikey," she said. under her breath.

Jesse dropped the cup on the floor. The handle broke off. She was sorry as soon as it happened. It's too late now, she said to herself. The cup is already broken. Boy, is Mom going to be mad! Mikey's going to cry. What is Dad going to say?

Jesse put the broken handle in the cup. She opened a kitchen drawer. It was full of papers and rubber bands. Jesse put the cup in the drawer and pushed it to the back. She covered it up with papers. She would tell her parents that she couldn't find the clown cup. She would say that it was lost. Jesse continued to set the table.

Mikey cried at dinner that night. Everyone looked for the clown cup. But nobody could find it. Jesse felt terrible.

5.

"Ready?" her mother asked.

"I'm ready," Jesse said. Her face was washed and her hair was brushed. She wore her good shorts, white sandals and her favorite white blouse.

"I'm ready, too," Mikey called. He ran to the front door. "Don't leave me!" he shouted.

Jesse's mother laughed. "We're not going to leave you," she said. She inspected her two children to make sure they were clean, dressed and buttoned. She checked Mikey's shoes to make sure they were on the correct feet. She opened the front door and they stepped out onto the porch. Then, they began to walk down the sidewalk.

Today was shopping day. On one Saturday of each month, Mother, Jesse, and Mikey rode a bus downtown. Dad stayed home and did work around the house. Today he was going to mow the lawn and paint the shutters. "Bye!" he called to them from the front yard.

"Bye, Daddy!" they called back.

"We'll be home soon," Jesse's mother said.

Jesse thought about what it was like being downtown. There were giant buildings. Hot dog vendors stood on street corners. Children ran after pigeons. The air smelled of cars, people and popcorn. Today would be fun and exciting. Even if she didn't have enough money to buy anything, she loved to look. There was so much to see!

As they walked, Jesse thought of the fun she would have riding up escalators, riding down escalators and looking in glass windows that held diamonds or silk scarves or chocolates.

But first they had to walk to the bus stop. It was several blocks away.

"I'm going to buy a 'copter," Mikey suddenly informed them.

"A what?" his mother asked.

"A 'copter," Mikey said. "So I can fly in the sky." He spun around in a circle.

"He means a helicopter," Jesse said. "How much money do you have?" she asked Mikey. "Helicopters cost a lot."

"I have a nickel," Mikey said. He reached into his pocket with his chubby hand. He pulled out a nickel and proudly showed it to Jesse. "I saved it," he said. "It's mine."

Jesse was just about to tell Mikey how dumb he was, when she noticed where they were. Jesse cautiously looked around for the gray dog. She sighed with relief when she saw the dog was nowhere in sight. They had almost reached Old Man Camber's Woods. They had to pass by the woods to reach the bus stop. This was the one part about trips to the city that Jesse didn't like.

It was scary to be so close to the woods, even in the daylight, because of all the stories she'd heard. She was glad her mother was with her. If Old Man Camber's ghost jumped out at them, she wouldn't be alone.

"Here's where Daddy found Mr. Bump," Mikey said. "Mr. Bump used to live here. He lived in a tree. He lived in a tree and he rode in a 'copter."

"Frogs don't live in trees. And they don't fly helicopters," Jesse said quietly.

"Do, too," Mikey said.

"Do not," Jesse said quickly.

"Children!" their mother cried. "For heaven's sake. Let's not fight. Let's have a nice afternoon. We're almost to the bus stop."

She was right. Jesse looked ahead and saw the bus stop. They had passed the woods. Jesse breathed a sigh of relief.

They waited at the bus stop for just a few minutes before the bus came. It was big and silver with a red stripe down its side.

"Hello there," said the driver. "Climb aboard. There's plenty of room."

Mother, Jesse, and Mikey climbed the steps. They walked down a little aisle then squeezed into a double seat together. Mikey sat on his mother's lap. The driver closed the door and the bus pulled back onto the road. They were headed toward the city.

Jesse liked to ride buses. She thought the different people on the bus looked interesting. Some people looked very old. She noticed mothers holding little, tiny babies. A few passengers looked like they'd just woken up. And some of the people looked like they knew wonderful stories about faraway places. Jesse gazed at the faces around her as the bus sped toward town.

"Elm Street's next," Jesse's mother said. "That's where we want to get off."

"Let me pull the bell! Let me pull the bell!" Mikey pleaded.

Several old ladies sitting near them smiled. "Isn't he darling?" one of them said.

Jesse wondered to herself why old people always

thought Mikey was so darling. They wouldn't think he was so darling if they lived with him, she thought. They wouldn't think he was so darling if they saw him eating pizza and getting tomato sauce all over his face and clothes.

Mikey stood on the seat while his mother held his waist so he wouldn't fall. He reached for a string over the window and pulled it. Ping! A little bell rang. Mikey smiled. "I pulled the bell!" he cried.

Jesse liked to pull the bell, too. It made her feel grown up. She would do it on the way home since Mikey got to do it on the way to the city.

"Elm Street!" called out the bus driver. The bus stopped. Mother, Jesse, and Mikey got off.

Jesse looked around. There weren't any buildings like this near her home. These buildings were so big and Jesse felt so little. But she kind of liked the feeling. It was an adventure.

"Let's go to the fabric store first," Jesse's mother said. "I need some thread."

Her mother held Mikey's hand. Jesse was eleven years old and too old for hand-holding. She was careful not to fall behind as she walked beside her mother. There were a lot of people on the sidewalk and she didn't want to get lost in the crowd.

First, they went to the fabric store for thread.

Next they went to a bakery for an apple coffee cake. On their way, they looked in the windows of a jewelry store and a dress shop.

"Let's go to the department store now," Jesse's mother said.

"Great!" That's what Jesse had been waiting for. She knew that the department store had everything in it. It had escalators, too. Jesse loved to ride the moving stairs, up and down.

In the department store they stopped on the sixth floor to look at women's dresses.

"Isn't this pretty?" Jesse's mother asked. She held up a white summer dress. The buttons on the front looked like little red cherries. "I think I'll try it on," she said. "Now you two wait right here. And don't you move from this spot. I don't want to lose you," she smiled.

Mikey started to walk away into the crowd. His mother grabbed his arm. "Jesse," she said. "You'd better hold Mikey's hand. He'll wander off if you don't."

"Aw, Mom." Jesse frowned and looked down at Mikey. "Do I have to?" she asked.

"Please, honey. I'll just be a minute." Jesse's mother hurried off to the dressing room.

Jesse stood still, holding Mikey's hand. She

listened to the noises of the crowd around her. She watched people walking back and forth across the floor and in and out among the racks of clothes. She held tightly onto Mikey's hand so that he couldn't pull away.

Suddenly, Jesse's stomach felt heavy. "Oh, no," she whispered under her breath. She dropped Mikey's hand. But, it was too late. *They* had already seen her! *They* were Sandy and Lisa, two older girls who used to go to Jesse's school. They were in the store and they were walking toward Jesse!

Sandy and Lisa were in the seventh grade in Junior High! Sandy wore panty hose. Lisa had pierced ears. Jesse thought they were neat. Jesse hoped she could be just as neat some day. And she hoped that they would talk to her. But not here . . . not now.

Jesse could feel her face flush pink. The two neatest girls in the school had seen her holding hands with her baby brother. What could be worse? Jesse groaned to herself.

Mikey started to walk away. "Come back here," Jesse said.

"No! I wanna go," Mikey said. "I'm tired of this place. I wanna go home."

Jesse grabbed his hand. Mikey tried to pull away.

Jesse held his hand tighter. Oh, no, she thought. Here they come. They see me.

Sandy and Lisa came nearer. They both looked at Jesse. Sandy pointed and Lisa giggled.

They're laughing at me, Jesse thought. "Hi, Sandy. Hi, Lisa," she said.

"Is that your boyfriend?" Sandy asked. She looked at Mikey and started giggling again.

"He's kind of young for you, isn't he?" Lisa said.

"He's my brother," Jesse said. "He's only five." She shrugged her shoulders. "I have to hold his hand or he'll wander away. Little brothers can be such a pain," she said. Jesse looked at Sandy and Lisa hoping that they would agree with her.

"Why did you bring him?" Sandy asked.

"My Mom's trying something on," Jesse said. "I'm just watching him for a minute."

"You mean you're here with your *mother*?" Sandy asked.

Jesse nodded.

"Can't you go shopping by yourself?" Lisa asked. "*We* came down by ourselves. I haven't shopped with my mother in *years*."

"Me neither," agreed Sandy.

Suddenly, Jesse was even more embarrassed. These girls were only two years older than she. Jesse felt like such a baby.

Mikey looked at Sandy and Lisa with curious brown eyes. "You rat face," he said to the two girls.

"Wh-what?" stammered Lisa.

"You rat face," Mikey said again. "Go away."

"Well!" Sandy said. "You're little brother is

really gross." She turned to Lisa and said, "Let's get out of here."

"Wait! He's only five years old!" Jesse called after them. "He doesn't know any better."

Sandy and Lisa disappeared into the crowd.

Jesse looked at Mikey. She wanted to spank him or push him or something. "You brat! Why did you say that?" she asked. "Why?"

"I don't like them," Mikey said. "They're mean."

"How can you not like them?" Jesse said. "You don't even know them." Jesse thought about it. Come to think of it, she said to herself, I don't like them either. And they were mean. They shouldn't have called her little brother gross, even if he was. They shouldn't have made her feel embarrassed to be with her mother. That wasn't very nice. Hm-m-m-m, Jesse thought. Maybe Mikey's not so dumb after all.

"What did you call them?" Jesse asked. She wanted to hear him say it again.

"Rat face," Mikey said. "Lisa rat face and Sandy rat face." He began to giggle.

"That's funny," she said between giggles.

Their mother walked up. "What are you two laughing about?" she asked.

"Rat face," said Mikey.

"What? Well, never mind." Mother hung the dress back on the rack. "It doesn't fit," she said with a sigh. "It's just as well, though. I don't really need a new dress. But, those cherry buttons are so cute." She smiled at Jesse and Mikey. "I'm glad to see you two getting along so well," she said. She took the hand of each child. With Mother in the middle, the three of them rode the escalator together, holding hands. It felt good and Jesse didn't care if anyone saw them.

*   *   *   *   *

Jesse, Mikey, and their mother stood by the bus stop on the sidewalk outside the department store. The bus pulled up. This time a different driver opened the door. Mother, Jesse, and Mikey climbed the steps, then they took a seat in the middle of the bus. Jesse sat by the window and looked out as the bus began to pull out into the city traffic.

Jesse looked up at the huge buildings as the bus slowly rolled by. They left the city and passed some houses, then some trees, then a farm. Cows stood in a meadow watching as the silver bus drove by.

"We're almost home," Jesse's mother said.

"I wanna pull the bell! I wanna pull the bell,"

60

Mikey shouted. Other people on the bus turned their heads to see who was making all the noise. "Sh-sh-sh!" Jesse's mother said. "Don't shout. You can pull the bell."

"But, Mom!" Jesse cried. "It's *my* turn. Mikey got to do it this morning. It's my turn now!"

"Oh, Jesse," her mother said as she shook her head. She looked tired. "Let Mikey pull the bell, all right? Let's not make a scene on the bus," she whispered. "Please?"

"I wanna pull the bell! I wanna pull the bell!" Mikey shouted. His face began to turn red.

"Sh-sh-sh," his mother warned. "Be quiet. You can pull the bell."

"Yea!" said Mikey. "I get to pull the bell!"

Jesse's mother held him while he reached across Jesse to the string. Ping! went the bell. Mikey smiled and laughed.

Jesse leaned her forehead against the window. She pretended she was looking outside so no one would see the tears in her eyes. "It's not fair," Jesse whispered. "It's just not fair."

6.

Jesse's ears were filled with the sound of rain drumming against the roof. The drops fell endlessly.

Inside the house, Jesse felt as if she was in a box. She couldn't play outside because it was too wet. She couldn't see much out of the windows because trickles of water slid down the glass. The rain was so heavy that she couldn't even see the mailbox at the end of the driveway.

Oh, no, she thought. One whole afternoon alone with Mikey. I don't know if I can stand it. I might go crazy.

Her mother and father walked into the room. Jesse's father buttoned up his black raincoat. "Keep an eye on Mikey while we're gone, okay?" he said. "I hope the house will still be standing when we get back." He winked at Jesse.

"Now, honey," her mother said. "You and Mikey have a nice time. There are popsicles in the freezer. But, don't let Mikey have more than one. Too many popsicles make him sick."

"Even one would make me sick," Jesse's dad said. "I don't know how you kids can eat that junk. If you want a snack, there's a bag of pumpkin seeds in the cabinet."

Jesse hid a smile behind her hand. Only her dad would eat pumpkin seeds for a snack, she thought. He always said that his health food kept him looking young. But, Jesse couldn't see any difference. He looked like a regular dad to her.

Jesse's mom took a red umbrella out of the hall closet. "I've left Mrs. Reed's number on the notepad by the telephone. We'll be back around three o'clock or so. Got that?"

Jesse looked worried.

"There's always Mrs. Willis next door if you need anything," her mother said. "But, I'm sure you'll be fine. How about a kiss?"

Jesse walked forward. Her mother stooped to kiss her on the cheek. Jesse understood that sometimes her mother liked to kiss her goodbye. Jesse didn't know how to tell her mother that, since she's eleven now, she is too old for that. She didn't want to hurt her mother's feelings. So Jesse let her do it, as long as it wasn't in front of Jesse's friends.

"Me! Me!" shouted Mikey. He ran to his mother

and held his arms in the air. "Kiss me, too!" he cried.

Jesse's mother laughed. "Okay, okay," she said. "A big kiss for a little boy." She kissed him.

"You too, Daddy," Mikey said.

Jesse's father lifted Mikey up and kissed him on the cheek.

What a baby, Jesse thought. I would never ask Dad to kiss me, even if I wanted him to.

"All right. Now you kids be good," Jesse's dad said. "Winkypopper, you mind your sister. Hear me? Stardoodle, keep an eye on your brother."

Jesse's father opened the front door. He held the red umbrella in one hand. Jesse's mother held onto his other arm. They stepped out into the rain and walked quickly to the car in the driveway. Jesse and Mikey stood at the window and watched them drive away. Jesse waved even though she knew her parents couldn't see her through all the rain. Mikey waved, too.

Jesse looked around the living room. What was there to do? Rainy days always made her feel a little tired. These days were perfect for sitting quietly and reading a book. Jesse thought of the horse book she had. She hadn't finished it, yet. Now would be a good time.

"What are you going to do?" Mikey asked.

"Read," said Jesse.

"What are you reading?" he asked.

"Horses," Jesse said as she took her book from under the couch where she'd left it.

"I like horses," Mikey said. "I want to be a horse when I grow up."

"That's dumb," Jesse said. "You can't be a horse."

"Why not?" Mikey looked puzzled.

"Because you're a boy," she added.

"I'll be a boy horse," Mikey said, smiling again. "Read to me," he pleaded. "Read to me about horses."

Jesse knew what it was like to read to Mikey. He kept interrupting her. He had to turn all the pages by himself. Sometimes when he turned the pages, he ripped them.

"No," Jesse said. "Get your own book."

"But, I can't read," Mikey reminded her. "I don't know how, yet."

"Quit bothering me," Jesse demanded. "Can't you go play by yourself?"

"Okay," Mikey said. "I'll play outside." He headed for the front door.

"No!" Jesse said. "It's raining. You'll catch cold

and then I'll get in trouble."

"I wanna play outside," Mikey whined. "I'm going to and you can't stop me!" He began to run. But, Jesse ran faster and reached the door first. As Mikey tugged at the door knob, Jesse turned the lock above his head. Once again, being the tallest came in handy.

"I wanna play outside," Mikey pleaded. His eyes began to fill with tears. His face was turning pink. Jesse could tell he was getting ready to throw a tantrum. She had to think of something fast, some way to get his attention.

"Why don't you draw?" Jesse suggested. "I'll get you some paper and magic markers. You can work on the kitchen table."

"Yea!" Mikey cheered. "Let's draw!" Playing outside was forgotten and his eyes sparkled with excitement.

"I'll read. You draw." Jesse took paper from the scrap paper bag. Daddy brought paper home from work. The paper usually had writing on one side. But, the other side was clean and just right for Mikey's scribblings. Her dad explained, "We're using this paper twice: first on one side at the office, then on the other side at home. Just think! We're saving a tree! We don't waste things in this house!"

On the outside of the bag the words SAVE A TREE had been printed by Jesse's dad. Jesse was glad that her parents were the type of people who cared about trees and flowers. But sometimes, she wondered if they cared about their eleven-year-old daughter who might be going crazy because of her five-year-old brother. She wondered if maybe they should have a SAVE JESSE bag. They could put Mikey in it and throw it away. Jesse smiled thinking about it.

Jesse went to the SAVE A TREE bag. She took out several sheets of paper and put them on the kitchen table. Next, she opened the cabinet under the sink. The magic markers were kept there in an orange juice can. There were many different colors: red, green, blue, orange, purple, brown, black, pink and yellow.

Mikey put a telephone book on the kitchen chair. On top of that he put a pillow. Then, he climbed up and sat on top of them. "What should I draw?" he asked.

"I don't know," Jesse said.

"I'll draw a rainbow." Mikey grabbed the blue marker. He drew large wiggly circles. Mikey's rainbow spilled off the sides of the paper onto the table.

"Stay on the paper," Jesse warned him.

"Now, I'll use pink," he said. He drew more wobbly lines.

"Stay on the paper!" Jesse said more loudly.

"I am," Mikey said.

"You are not! Look!" She lifted the paper and pointed to the table. Blue and pink lines sprawled here and there.

"Give it back," Mikey said, reaching for the paper that Jesse held.

"Will you stay on the paper?" she asked.

"Yes," Mikey answered.

"Promise?" Jesse asked him.

"I promise," Mikey said, smiling.

Jesse returned the paper to Mikey. "This is a wonderful, wonderful rainbow," he said. "Now, I'll use green."

Jesse left Mikey to his drawing. She walked to the family room and sat down on the couch. Rat-a-tat went the rain on the roof.

Jesse opened her horse book and began reading. She could hear Mikey talking to himself in the kitchen. "This is a very beautiful color," he said. "I better put some here. I missed a spot."

Jesse smiled. Mikey can be pretty funny sometimes, she thought. He was okay when he was being good. But when he was bad, he was a super pain. Jesse frowned just thinking about it.

Jesse heard Mikey's voice from the kitchen again. "Orange and red," he said. "This is the most beautiful picture that I've ever done. It's the most beautiful picture in the world. Everyone can see it and know I did it." There was silence again which meant that Mikey was working hard on his rainbow.

Jesse smiled. She returned to her book. She was reading about a type of western horse called an Appaloosa. This type of horse had a spotted hide and the Indians rode it. It was a very strong horse.

Rain continued to fall. Rat-a-tat.

"Look!" Mikey said excitedly. He ran up to Jesse and held his drawing out for her to see. A mass of scribbles covered the page. A snarl of green and blue on top of red and yellow spread over the paper.

"Which is your favorite color?" Mikey asked.

Jesse stared at the scribbles. "The green," she said, thinking that his picture didn't look at all like a rainbow.

Mikey nodded his head in agreement. "That's my favorite, too."

"Help me put it up where Mommy and Daddy can see it," he said. "Please?"

"Oh, all right." Jesse put down her book and

stood up. She walked with Mikey to the kitchen. On the refrigerator Mikey's and Jesse's artwork was displayed. They used scotch tape and magnets to hold up the drawings on the refrigerator. She looked on the refrigerator door to see if there was room for the rainbow drawing.

"Use that one," Mikey said. He pointed to a magnet shaped like a ladybug. It was out of his reach. The magnet held one of Jesse's pictures, a picture of a race horse.

Jesse sighed. There was no point in arguing with him, she reasoned. He'll just cry until he gets his way. Jesse took her picture down. She placed Mikey's drawing in that spot. The ladybug magnet held his picture in place.

"No," Mikey said. His face fell into a pout. "I want it to go there, up higher." He pointed again at the refrigerator door. "I want it where everyone can see it."

What a baby, Jesse thought. She moved a finger-painting to make room for the rainbow. Mikey stared at it, then said, "That's good right there. It looks nice. I can't wait for Mommy and Daddy to see it!"

"Can I read now?" Jesse asked. "Can you be quiet long enough so I can read?"

"I want a popsicle," Mikey said. "Mommy said I could have one. I want a red one."

"All right, but just one. And don't make a mess." Jesse opened the freezer and took a cherry popsicle out of a box. "You have to sit at the table," she said.

Mikey ran to the kitchen table and climbed onto his chair. Perched on top of the telephone book and the cushion, he yelled, "I wanna popsicle! I wanna popsicle!"

Jesse gave the red popsicle to her little brother. She looked at the kitchen table for the first time and cried out, "Oh! Mikey!"

The table was covered with scribbles, all colors of scribbles: red, orange, green, blue, yellow, purple, brown, black and pink. An explosion of wiggly lines covered the end of the table where Mikey had been drawing.

"What's wrong?" Mikey asked. He sucked on the top of his popsicle. His teeth were turning pink from the cherry color.

"Look at the mess you made!" Jesse said. "Now I have to clean it up! Why did you draw on the table?"

"I didn't," said Mikey. "I stayed on the paper."

"Then you must be blind," Jesse said. "Look at that table! It's a mess!"

"It's pretty," said Mikey. "It's a rainbow."

Jesse took a sponge and a can of cleanser. She scrubbed the table. As she scrubbed, she said to herself, He's driving me nuts. He's driving me nuts.

After several minutes of scrubbing, she could hardly see the magic marker lines. Maybe Mom and Dad wouldn't notice. Jesse hoped not. She rinsed out the sponge at the sink, then turned around to see how Mikey was doing with the popsicle.

"Mikey!" she exclaimed. "Your shirt!"

Mikey had two red streaks on the front of his shirt. His mouth looked like a clown's with an inch of cherry-red skin surrounding his lips.

"What a mess!" Jesse said. "I told you to be careful. Now Mom's going to be mad at me."

Jesse took a fresh paper towel. She wet it under the faucet. Armed with the moist paper, she scrubbed around Mikey's mouth.

"Ow!" he yelled. "You're hurting me!"

The last chunk of red ice on Mikey's popsicle began to slide down the stick. Jesse caught it in her hand before it fell to the floor.

"That's mine," Mikey said. He took the popsicle piece from Jesse's hand and popped it into his mouth.

"Can I have another one?" Mikey asked. "I want an orange one now."

"No," said Jesse. "Mom said you could only have one."

Mikey's eyes began to fill with tears. "Please?" he said. "Just one more? I promise I won't make a mess. Please?"

"No," Jesse said firmly. "If you have another one your stomach might freeze up. And if your stomach freezes, then your legs will freeze, too. You won't be able to walk."

One good thing about little brothers is that they'll believe anything, Jesse thought.

"I don't care," Mikey said. "I don't care if my stomach freezes. I *want* my stomach to freeze."

"But your legs will freeze, too," Jesse fibbed. She was beginning to worry. He wasn't falling for the freezing story. "Your legs will freeze and you won't be able to walk," Jesse said. "*Then* what would you do?"

"I could ride in a 'copter. I could ride in a 'copter with Mr. Bump. Please?" Mikey whined. "Just one more. I want an orange one."

Jesse closed her eyes for a second, then opened them. She was so tired of fighting with him. "Okay," she said. "Just one more. And you better not tell Mom. If you do I'll tell her you made a mess with the magic markers."

"I won't tell," Mikey promised. "I want an orange one."

Jesse gave Mikey a popsicle. She watched him while he ate. She caught pieces that fell from the stick. And she tried to wipe the orange popsicle spots off of his shirt.

"Now let me read," Jesse said. "You be quiet while I read. Go take a nap or something. Go play somewhere."

"Will you read to me?" Mikey asked.

"No. Go play and be quiet. And don't get into trouble," Jesse ordered. Mikey left the room.

Good, Jesse thought. He's going back to his bedroom. He'll play there for a while and leave me alone.

Jesse opened her book again. The next chapter was about Palominos. They were horses from Arabia. The picture in the book showed a beautiful, creamy golden-colored horse. Its mane and tail were snow-white. The horse stood on top of a hill. The wind fluttered its mane and tail.

Jesse wondered what it would be like to own a horse like that. She could keep it in the backyard and it could eat grass. Then, her father wouldn't have to mow the lawn anymore. She would name her horse Butterscotch.

Jesse thought about riding the horse to school. She would stop for Karen and Biff. All three of them could fit on Butterscotch's back. Then Butterscotch would gallop like the wind. If a dog ran out to bark at them, Butterscotch would step on its tail. If a ghost from Old Man Camber's Woods came out to get them, Butterscotch would jump right over that ghost.

Jesse looked at the picture of the Palomino. She daydreamed and smiled to herself. She and Butterscotch could join a circus. They would do tricks and jump through hoops of fire. People would cheer. Butterscotch would wear a big pink feather on his head. She would wear a sparkling silver costume with golden boots. She would . . .

C R A S H !

The sound came from down the hall. Jesse jumped up and ran. She heard Mikey crying in her bedroom. When she reached her room, she stopped and let out a cry.

The crash she had heard was her doll shelf. The shelf, with all her dolls from around the world, had fallen off of the wall. Her dolls lay in a tangle on the floor. An overturned chair lay there, too. Mikey sat crying on the floor beside the chair.

"What did you do?" Jesse yelled angrily. "Get

out of my room! You ruined my dolls! Get out! Get out!"

Mikey sat on the floor and cried.

"Mikey, I hate you!" she yelled. "I hate you!" Jesse knew somewhere inside that she shouldn't say that. But, she couldn't help it. Mikey is such a brat, such a terrible, terrible brother! she thought. He breaks things. He tears things. He spills things. He scribbles on things. He lies. He makes messes. He cries.

Jesse looked at her dolls lying in a jumbled up mess on the floor. Out of the mess, little china legs and arms stuck out. Silk and satin dresses were crumpled. Ponytails and braids lay this way and that way.

All of my beautiful, beautiful dolls are probably broken, she moaned to herself. I've worked so hard collecting them. I've taken such good care of them. And WHO had to ruin them? WHO had to break them? WHO ELSE?

MIKEY! Mikey the creep. Mikey the brat. Mikey the worst, most awful, most terrible brother in the world! Jesse thought, trying to hold back her tears.

Jesse looked at Mikey. He sat on the floor beside the fallen dolls. His face was flushed. He was crying as loudly as he could. But, she didn't care.

Jesse picked up her doll from Spain. Its hair was messed up, but at least it wasn't broken. She carefully laid the doll on her bed.

Jesse heard the front door open. "What's all the noise about?" she heard her father say.

"Jesse? Mikey? Are you all right?" her mother called. She ran back to Jesse's bedroom.

"My heavens," her mother said. "What happened? Mikey, are you all right? Come here, honey."

Mikey ran to his mother. She picked him up and held him while he sobbed on her shoulder.

"He broke my shelf!" Jesse yelled. "He broke it. He broke all my dolls!"

"Oh, Mikey," Mother said. "Did you do this?"

"I didn't mean to," Mikey mumbled into his mother's neck. "I didn't mean to break anything. I just wanted to see the dolls."

"Mikey, you should never, never touch Jesse's dolls unless she says you can," Jesse's father said. He was using his deep voice which meant he was angry.

"But, I just wanted to see them," Mikey sobbed. "I didn't mean to hurt anything."

"Well, let's see what the damage is," Jesse's mother said. She looked at the wooden shelf lying on the floor. "I can fix this without too much trouble," she said.

"Don't worry, Stardoodle," said Jesse's dad. "We'll get your dolls all fixed up again."

Jesse felt like crying when her dad called her Stardoodle. He was trying to be so nice. But, she couldn't be nice back to him right now. She was too angry. She had the worst little brother in the world. And all her dolls were lying in a heap on the floor. She was so mad she felt like breaking something. But the only thing she could think to break was Mikey.

Jesse's dad picked up a doll. "Miss Japan looks okay," he said. "You can't even tell she took a tumble." He set her on the bed beside the Spanish doll. "And Miss Scotland looks good," he said. "She's still holding on to her bagpipe."

Jesse picked up a doll and closely looked at it. What a relief! Miss Switzerland wasn't broken. And neither was Miss Denmark.

"Miss Ireland and Miss Belgium look in pretty good shape," said her dad.

Mikey stopped sobbing. Still in his mother's arms, he turned his head and watched his father pick up the dolls. His thumb was in his mouth. His eyes were red from crying.

"Miss Italy looks okay," her dad said. He set her

on the bed. "So is Miss Germany."

"Miss Egypt is okay," Jesse said. "Miss England's hair is messed up."

"We'll fix her hair," said her mother. "Don't worry. We'll iron the dolls' skirts, too."

"That just leaves two more," said her dad. "Here's Miss Norway. She's missing a shoe. Better look under the bed."

Jesse crawled under her bed. There was the shoe. As she grabbed it, she noticed something else under there in the dark and dust. It was little, about the size of a walnut. Jesse squirmed over to see it. "Oh, no!" she cried.

"What is it?" her parents asked.

"It's Nicole's head!" Jesse howled.

"The doll from France?" her mother asked.

"Yes!" Jesse, holding Nicole's little head in her hand, wiggled out from under the bed. "Look!" she said as she glared at Mikey. Then she choked back a sob.

Jesse opened her hand for everyone to see. In her palm lay Nicole's little china head. Her painted blue eyes still stared and her little red mouth still smiled.

Mikey began to cry again. He hid his face against his mother's neck.

"She's broken," Jesse said quietly. "Nicole is broken." Jesse picked Nicole's body up from the floor. The yellow silk dress didn't look so pretty without the smiling china face above it. "Nicole is ruined," Jesse said. "She's ruined forever."

In a daze, Jesse looked at Nicole's body in one hand and the little china head in her other hand. She felt the same feeling she got when she saw a dead bird, especially a robin. Once when she was walking to school, Jesse had seen a robin under a bush. It was so pretty. Its breast feathers were orangey-red. She looked at it more closely and she saw it was dead. It was such a pretty little thing and lying so still. It had seemed awful and sad when she saw that robin. And that's the feeling Jesse had now when she looked at Nicole.

A big tear squeezed out of Jesse's eye. It trickled down her nose and fell to the floor beside the broken doll shelf.

"Now wait just a minute, Stardoodle," her father said. "Let me see that."

Jesse handed him the two pieces of Nicole. He carefully looked at both parts. "This is a clean break," he said. "I think we can glue her together. Yes, I know we can. We'll use Super Glue. It works on china. That stuff works on anything." He patted Jesse on the head. "We'll fix her right up."

"Really?" Jesse asked. She perked up for a second. Then she looked sad once more. "But, she'll never be the same again," she said. "It'll show on her neck where you glue it."

"Hm-m-m-m," her father said. He scratched his chin.

"Wasn't she wearing a pearl necklace?" her

mother asked. "That would cover the break."

Jesse looked around her room. She spotted the tiny pearl necklace lying in the corner where it had fallen. Jesse picked it up. "Yes," she said. "I think it will cover the break."

"Great!" Jesse's father said. "All we need is a little Super Glue and Nicole will be as good as new. I'll get some at the store tomorrow." He smiled. "Cheer up, Buttercup. Things are never quite as bad as they seem. Every cloud has a silver lining."

My dad is always saying stuff like that, Jesse thought. He means well. But, he must not know what it's like to have a little brother like Mikey.

Jesse glared at Mikey. He stood close beside his mother holding onto her skirt.

"I'm just glad it wasn't any worse than this," Jesse's mother said. She looked down at Mikey. "Young man," she said. "You're going to bed early tonight. And I think you owe your sister an apology. Are you sorry for what you did?"

Mikey hung his head. "Yes," he said quietly. "I'm sorry."

Mother looked more closely at Mikey. "Michael Vincent Andrews," she said. "You're a mess! It's bath time for you. How can you get so dirty in one afternoon?"

Mikey looked up with big brown eyes. "Jesse gave me two popsicles," he said. "Orange and red." He pointed to the orange spots and the red streaks on his shirt.

"What?" his mother said. She seemed surprised. She looked at Jesse as she shook her head. Then she smiled. "Don't worry, honey," she said. "I'm not going to yell. I think we've had enough excitement for one day. Let's all try to calm down."

Jesse was relieved. Sometimes her mom surprised her. She seemed to know when Jesse felt like she was ready to pop or scream or something.

Jesse's mom took Mikey by the hand and turned to her husband. "Gary, would you start dinner, please, while I bathe Mikey? Then we can all have a nice quiet evening."

"Sure, hon. Soyburgers and alfalfa sprouts coming up!" Jesse's dad headed for the kitchen. Her mother and Mikey left for the bathroom. Jesse heard the bath tub filling up with water.

Jesse closed her door. Alone in her room, she looked at her dolls. Her father had taken Nicole. The other dolls lay in a neat row on her bed. Jesse knelt on the floor beside them. She patted Miss Ireland and Miss Germany on the head.

"You know, you're all very lucky," Jesse whispered to the twelve dolls. "You're lucky you don't have a little brother. You're lucky you don't have to be a big sister. And you're lucky not to be the oldest kid in the house. It's terrible! It's awful! No one understands how bad it is to have a baby brother."

Jesse laid her head on the bed and closed her eyes.

It had been a long, rainy afternoon. The raindrops still drummed against the roof.

"It's just not fair," Jesse mumbled.

7.

The next day Jesse's dad came home with Super Glue. It was in a little silver tube. Jesse watched her dad while he fixed Nicole's head. He put a few drops of the clear glue on the broken edge. Then he pressed Nicole's head against the neck. Some glue squeezed out from between the two pieces. He wiped it off, then put a piece of tape around her neck. This was to hold it in place while it dried.

Her dad gave Nicole to Jesse. "Now put her somewhere safe," he said. "The glue dries pretty fast. She'll be as good as new in no time at all." He squeezed Jesse's hand and smiled.

Jesse was glad she had the kind of father who squeezed hands. She wanted to do something extra nice for him. She wanted him to know how she felt. What could she do to show him? Jesse thought about it.

"Dad," Jesse said. "I'm going to try to eat

pumpkin seeds every day for the rest of my life."

Jesse's dad looked surprised. He had a wide smile. "What in the world for?" he asked.

"Because you said it's good for me," Jesse said.

"That's fine, Jess. But, don't push yourself too hard," her dad said. "You don't have to eat pumpkin seeds every day. But while you're at it, you might try a little tofu, too."

Just thinking about tofu, that gross, cottage-cheesey stuff, made Jesse feel sick. "Okay," she said. "I'll try it again."

Jesse figured she better get out of the kitchen fast before her father got her to promise to eat any more weird stuff.

Jesse took Nicole back to her bedroom. Her mother was there. She was hanging the repaired shelf on the wall. "I think this should do it," she said proudly. She stepped back and looked at the shelf. "Pretty good, even if I do say so myself." She picked up Miss Spain and set her on the shelf.

"I'll do that, Mom," Jesse said. "I know where they all go."

"Okay." Her mom put the hammer and nails back into the tool box. She looked down at Jesse. "Are you still angry at your brother?" she asked.

Jesse thought for a minute. She knew she was

still angry, but she was too ashamed to admit it.

"I'm trying not to be," Jesse said.

"Well, that's good." Her mother smiled. "You know, Jess. He's only five years old. He just doesn't know any better."

Jesse felt herself getting a little more angry. She'd heard this so many times before. Her heart beat faster. "But, it's not fair," she said. "Mikey gets away with everything. He gets to do anything he wants to do."

"Hm-m-m-m," Jesse's mother said. "It must seem that way sometimes. But, that's not really true." She sat beside Jesse on the edge of the bed and put her arm around Jesse's shoulders. "There are lots of things that Mikey wants to do. He wants to do the same things that you do. But, he can't because he's too young."

"Like what?" Jesse asked.

"Well, he'd like to read, but he can't," her mother said. "He'd like to go to school, but he's too young. He'd like to ride a bicycle, but he's too little. He'd like to reach the cabinet in the kitchen to get a drinking glass, but he's too short. He'd like to fly in a helicopter to the moon, too, but he doesn't understand that's impossible," Jesse's mother laughed. "There are lots of things that Mikey wants to do. But, he's only five years old. You know, Jess. Mikey wants to be more like *you*. He looks at you and sees a grown-up."

Jesse frowned. "But, he's such a pest!" she said. "He gets into my stuff. I feel more like his babysitter than his sister."

"I know," her mother said. "But, try to understand, honey. He's really pretty helpless in many ways. Why, he can't even take a bath by himself or tie his own shoes! Five years old isn't always an easy age."

"Neither is eleven," Jesse said.

Her mother gently pinched the end of Jesse's nose. "Thirty-six isn't always a picnic," she said. "But, it's what I am. And I have to make the best of it." She winked at Jesse. "Anyway," she said, "we've all got each other. That's something to be thankful for. Just think! When you're all grown up, you'll probably look back on these days and laugh."

Jesse was quiet. She didn't want to say anything out loud. She thought her mother might be wrong. She didn't think there was anything very funny about having a creep for a brother. And Nicole's broken head was no laughing matter . . . not today, not even ten years from now.

"I know you don't think it's very funny right now," her mother said.

Uh, oh, Jesse thought. Can she read my mind? Jesse squirmed on the bed. She looked down at the floor.

"Mikey will grow up before you know it," her mother said. "And your little brother won't be so little anymore." She sighed and patted Jesse's hand. "Time flies by quickly."

"Not for me it doesn't," Jesse said. "It seems like I've been a little girl forever."

Jesse got up from the bed. She put Miss Japan on the shelf next to Miss Spain.

"Mom?" she asked. "Do you think I'll ever like Mikey? I mean, do you think he'll always be a brat?"

Jesse's mother stood up. "Well, honey," she said. "I think what you're really asking is, 'Will Mikey always be five years old?'" She shook her head. "No, he won't be. He'll grow up just like you grew up. You know, you were five years old once, too." Jesse's mother grinned.

"I know," Jesse said.

"It's just a little hard for you right now," her mother said. "As the older child, you have more responsibilities."

I have about a million of them, Jesse thought to herself. I have a million responsibilities and they're all named Mikey.

8.

"Mom, is it okay if Karen and Biff come over tonight after dinner? We want to make some fudge. We don't even have to cook it. Biff says you just mix all the stuff together and put it in the refrigerator. She got the recipe from her grandmother." Jesse looked hopeful. "I've done my homework," she said.

"I don't know, honey," her mother said. "Your father and I were thinking of going for a drive after dinner. Don't you and Mikey want to come?"

"No!" Mikey shouted. He sat in a corner of the family room. He was surrounded by pillows. Every pillow in the house had been gathered, then stacked up to make the walls of his fort. Mikey worked very hard to place the pillows just right.

"No!" he shouted again. "I don't wanna go. I wanna stay here. I wanna make fudge with Jesse. I wanna help."

Mother looked at Jesse. "Will you watch him while we're gone?" she asked.

Jesse thought about it. The way she saw it, she had two choices. She could go on a boring drive with Mom, Dad, and Mikey. She would have to sit in the back seat with him. And sometimes he didn't stay on his side. Sometimes he got sick.

Or she could have Karen and Biff over to make fudge. Either way she had to put up with Mikey. At least she wouldn't be stuck in the back seat of a car with him if she stayed home.

"Okay," Jesse said. "He can stay."

"Yea! Yea! I'm gonna make some fudge!" Mikey yelled. "I wanna stir it up. Can I? Can I lick the bowl?"

"Maybe," said Jesse. "We'll see."

The family ate dinner, then cleaned up. Jesse's mom said, "We won't be gone long. You two have a nice time." She walked out of the door with Jesse's father. Just as Jesse's parents started the car, Biff and Karen strolled up the sidewalk. They all waved to each other. "Save me a piece of fudge," Jesse's mom called from the car window as they drove off.

"Hi. Come on in," Jesse called from the front door. "Mom and Dad are going for a drive," she said. "What's in the bag?" Jesse pointed at a paper bag in Biff's hand.

"I brought cocoa and vanilla," Biff said. "Karen

brought condensed milk. You have sugar and eggs, right?"

"Right," said Jesse. "Let's get started." They walked into the kitchen.

"Hi Biff Hi Karen Hi Biff Hi Karen Hi Biff Hi Karen." Mikey came running into the kitchen. "Can I help?"

"Yeah," said Jesse. "You can sit down and be quiet." The girls giggled.

"But, I wanna help," Mikey said. "Mommy said I could."

"No, she didn't," Jesse said.

"Did too," Mikey answered.

"Did not," Jesse said annoyingly.

"Did too," Mikey said, quietly.

"She did not. Leave us alone," Jesse said. "You always get in the way."

"You're mean!" Mikey wailed. He ran from the kitchen.

"Finally," Jesse said. "Some peace and quiet. Let's start. There's a mixing bowl over there."

Karen got the bowl. She cracked eggs into it, then added sugar. Biff poured a teaspoon of vanilla into the mixture. "Where's the cocoa?" she asked.

"Right here," said Jesse. She measured the cocoa, then poured it into the bowl. "Achoo!" she sneezed. "I got some in my nose," she said.

Mikey walked into the kitchen again. He held a big brown frog in his hands. "Me and Mr. Bump are gonna help," he said. "Mr. Bump knows about fudge. Mr. Bump makes fudge all the time."

"He does not," Jesse said. "Get him out of here."

"Yuk!" Karen wrinkled her nose. "I wouldn't eat any fudge a frog made. That's gross!"

"P.U.," said Biff. "Don't let that frog near the fudge."

Mikey pouted. "But, we wanna help. Mr. Bump can stir it up with his legs."

"Oh, gross!" said Jesse. "Mikey, you get that frog out of this kitchen right now. I mean it!"

"No," said Mikey. He had a stubborn look on his face. Jesse knew that he wouldn't budge from the kitchen. Here we go again, Jesse thought. He's trying to ruin my fun. He ruins *everything*. He rips my books. He ruins my slumber parties. He spills lemonade on my friends. He gets to pull the bell two times on the bus. I have to hold his hand when we go shopping. He breaks Nicole's head off. He breaks my doll shelf. He tells Mom I gave him two popsicles and now I want to make fudge and HE JUST WON'T LEAVE ME ALONE!

Jesse lost her temper. "Mikey!" she yelled. "I've

had it with you!" She ran across the kitchen floor and grabbed the frog from Mikey's hands.

"Give him back!" Mikey screamed.

"No," shouted Jesse. "I'm going to let him go. You and your dumb frog won't get out of the kitchen. So, I'm going to let Mr. Bump go. He's almost as big a pest as you are!"

Jesse opened the kitchen door. She set Mr. Bump outside under a bush. "Go home!" she yelled at the frog. "We don't want you here anymore!"

"He's mine," Mikey cried. "He's mine! Give him back! I want Mr. Bump!"

Jesse closed the door and locked it. "No," she said. "Mr. Bump doesn't live here anymore. Frogs don't belong in kitchens. Neither do pesty little brothers. Now, go to your room or I'll tell Mom and Dad how bad you were to bring a frog into the kitchen."

Mikey's eyes filled with tears. His shoulders shook as he sobbed. He turned and ran from the kitchen. Jesse heard a door slam. "You better not be in my room," she called after him.

Jesse turned back to Karen and Biff. They both stood, quietly watching. "I'm sorry, you guys," Jesse said. "He's such a pest. He'll leave us alone, now."

"I know what it's like," Karen said. "Remember, I have a little sister." She smiled at Jesse. "Kimmy isn't any better than Mikey. Believe me."

"Let's get this fudge finished," Biff said. "I have to be home before it gets dark outside." She looked at the recipe. "It says here 'a dash of salt.' How much is a dash?"

"I think a dash is the same as a pinch," said Karen. She dropped a pinch of salt into the bowl.

The three girls took turns stirring the fudge. It

got to be so thick that they could barely pull the spoon through it.

"Great! It's done," said Jesse. She spooned it into a buttered pan. Then she put the fudge in the refrigerator. "You guys come over tomorrow and we'll eat it," she said.

"O-o-o-o," Biff groaned. "I don't know if I can eat anymore. I ate a lot of the batter tonight while we were making it." She held her stomach. "Well, I'd better be going. It's getting dark outside."

"Me, too," said Karen. She anxiously looked out the window. The sky was just getting dark enough for a full moon to show.

"We'll see ya, Jess," Biff said.

"Bye," called Karen. They both left by the front door.

"Bye." Jesse waved. Then she went back to the kitchen to clean up. Mom and Dad should be home pretty soon, she thought.

Jesse suddenly remembered Mikey. She thought to herself, "He's been real good, nice and quiet. I'll give him a spoonful of fudge."

"Mikey!" Jesse called. "You can come out of your room now. Come and get some fudge."

There was no answer.

"Mikey!" Jesse yelled. "Come and get some

fudge! I'm not mad at you anymore!"

There was no answer.

Jesse felt a funny feeling in her stomach. Why wasn't Mikey answering?

Jesse walked back to his bedroom. She looked inside, but Mikey wasn't there. Maybe he's hiding, she thought. She looked under his bed and in the closet. She ran to her room. But, Mikey wasn't there either. Next, she checked her parents' bedroom, but no Mikey.

"Where is he? Where could he be?" Jesse said. "Oh, no!"

I know where he is, Jesse said to herself. He went to look for Mr. Bump! He must have sneaked out the front door. I'll bet he went to look for Mr. Bump under the bush by the kitchen door. That's where I let the frog go.

Jesse threw open the kitchen door. She looked under the bush, but there was no frog. She ran into the backyard. "Mikey!" she called. "Mikey, where are you?" It was dark now. The moon glowed white in a black sky.

"Oh, what should I do? What should I do?" Jesse whispered to herself. "He's not here. Oh, no. Where are Mom and Dad? They'll know what to do."

Jesse saw headlights shining through the darkness.

A car was driving up the road. "It's them! It's them!" Jesse said. She ran to the driveway. "Mom! Dad!" she called. "Mikey's gone. He's run away!"

"What?" Jesse's mother and father ran to her. "What's wrong? What happened?" they asked.

Jesse explained the whole story to them. She told how Mikey and Mr. Bump were in the kitchen. She told how Mikey wanted to put Mr. Bump in the bowl so he could kick the fudge. She explained that she put Mr. Bump outside. Mikey must have run away to look for him.

"Let's all calm down," her mother said. "He couldn't have gotten very far."

"But, it's so dark out," Jesse cried. "What if he can't find his way home?"

"Then we'll just have to find him," her dad said. "You stay here, Jesse, in case he comes home. Your mother and I will go look for him. We'll take the car. The headlights will help us."

"That's a good idea," her mother said. "Hurry, Gary! Let's go!"

Jesse's parents slowly drove down the road. Jesse heard her mother's voice calling Mikey from the window. Jesse watched as the car disappeared into the darkness. She walked back into the house and into the kitchen.

Jesse looked around. Everything seemed different now. Just a little while ago, she and Biff and Karen were laughing together. They were making fudge and having a good time. Now everything had fallen to pieces. Mikey was gone. Her parents were upset. It was all her fault.

"Oh, Jesse. What have you done?" she whispered to herself.

Jesse walked around the kitchen. The light was too bright. It hurt her eyes. She walked in circles. She began opening and closing drawers and cabinets just for something to do. She wanted to pass the time. But, all she could think of was Mikey.

She opened the cabinet under the sink. There were the magic markers in the orange juice can. She remembered the rainy afternoon that she and Mikey had spent together. He drew a rainbow. And she got mad at him for making a mess. She didn't want to remember that right now. So, she closed the cabinet.

Jesse walked in another circle around the kitchen. Then, she opened a drawer. Oh, no! What she saw in the drawer reminded her of Mikey.

It was the clown cup. The clown cup that *she* had broken and hidden. Jesse reached into the drawer and pulled out the cup. She remembered the day that she had broken it. She smiled thinking about Mr. Bump knocking over Jim's lemonade. She thought of the big, ugly frog sitting on Jim's arithmetic book. Boy, did Jim look surprised! Jesse giggled. I wonder if Mom was right? she thought. Maybe this will seem funny some day.

But, when Jesse looked at the broken clown cup again, that didn't seem so funny. Why did I do it? Why did I break it? The questions whirled in her mind. "I'm sorry," she whispered. "I'm sorry I broke my little brother's clown cup. He broke Nicole. But, he didn't break her on purpose. It was an accident."

Jesse thought of Nicole. With her head glued on she looked almost as good as new. Thank goodness for the Super Glue . . .

"Super Glue! That's it!" Jesse exclaimed.

She opened another drawer and took out a little silver tube. It said Super Glue on the label. She took the top off and squeezed a few drops onto the clown cup's broken handle. She pressed it against the cup. Then, she wrapped tape around it to hold it in place while it dried, just like her father did with Nicole's head.

The cup looked fine. Jesse put the cup on the table to dry. She looked inside it to see the smiling clown face with the bright red nose. Mikey would be so happy to see it if he ever came home. If he came back . . .

Wait a minute, Jesse thought. Why am I saying *if*? Mikey *will* come home. He *has* to come home. He's *got* to come home. This is all my fault!

Jesse sat at the table. She rested her head on her arms and cried. "Oh, Mikey," she said through her sniffling. "I'm sorry I put Mr. Bump out of the house. I'm sorry you're lost. Where did you go? Oh, where did you go?"

Soon, Jesse stopped crying. "This isn't getting me anywhere," she said. She blew her nose. "Now if I were a frog, where would I go? If I were Mikey, where would I think a frog would go?"

Jesse thought and thought. Suddenly, she sat up in her chair. She opened her eyes wide. "Oh, no!" she said. I know where Mikey went! she thought. He went to Old Man Camber's Woods. I told Mr. Bump to go home. Old Man Camber's Woods is Mr. Bump's home. Oh, no! Mikey's in the haunted woods with ghosts and bats and . . . and . . . who knows what else?

"I've got to do something," Jesse groaned. "I can't just sit here. I know where he is." She looked at the clock. Mom and Dad have been gone a long time, she thought. They probably won't come home until they find Mikey. They'll never guess that he's in Old Man Camber's Woods, never in a million years.

Jesse sighed. "There's just one thing for me to do," she said out loud. "I'll go to the haunted woods and find Mikey. I'll go there if it's the last thing I do!" She opened the kitchen door and looked out into the dark, dark night. A full moon shone in the distance behind the trees . . . Old Man Camber's trees.

Suddenly, Jesse felt cold. She buttoned up her sweater. Then, she began to walk through the darkness. She looked straight ahead as she came closer and closer to Old Man Camber's Woods.

Jesse stood up straight as she walked. "He's my brother," she said out loud to herself. "Mikey's my little brother. And he's only five years old."

9.

Jesse almost ran down the sidewalk. She had to hurry. She knew Mikey was alone in the woods. He was probably lost and afraid. Jesse put her hands in her pockets and walked quickly.

"Gr-r-r." From out of the darkness came the sound of a growling dog.

Jesse stopped and listened. She peered through the darkness. Then she saw it in the moonlight. A big, gray, fuzzy dog, the same dog that had snarled at her, Karen, and Biff on their way to school. Karen and Biff had saved her that day. But, they weren't here now. Jesse was on her own.

Jesse stood very still, watching. The dog crawled closer and closer. Its lips pulled back to show shining, pointed teeth.

Maybe I should run home, Jesse thought. She started to turn. But, then she remembered Mikey. She had to get past the dog so that she could get to the woods. She had to find Mikey.

Jesse stamped her foot on the ground. "Go

away!" she yelled. "Go away!"

The dog looked surprised. It stopped crawling toward her.

Jesse slowly backed away from the dog. When she couldn't see it anymore she turned around. She kept walking. She felt braver now. She had gotten by the dog! She would tell Biff and Karen . . . that is, if she ever saw them again. But, the hardest part was still to come . . . Old Man Camber's Woods.

The sidewalk became a dirt path. Jesse followed it in the moonlight. Then she walked by a tree, then another and another. Jesse was in Old Man Camber's Woods.

Jesse looked up into the sky. Above her the moon shone through the tree branches. The limbs looked like giant skeleton hands reaching over her. Leaves crunched under her feet as she walked among the trees.

"Who-o . . . Who-o."

What was that? Jesse asked herself, as her heart beat faster.

"Who-o." The sound came again. Jesse looked around to see what was making the noise. She saw an owl perched on a branch above her. It looked at her with round, wide eyes. It sat very still and said, "Whooo-o."

"I'm Jesse Andrews," Jesse said. "I've come to find my little brother. His name is Mikey and he's only five years old. Will you help me?"

The owl blinked its eyes. It stared at Jesse. "Animals always help people in fairy tales," Jesse said. "Will you help me?"

The owl just stared.

"Okay," Jesse said. "I guess I'll just have to find him by myself." She walked on.

Suddenly, Jesse heard the sound of something running through the leaves. It rustled through the dry weeds, quick little steps. Jesse caught her breath. She listened, but the sound stopped. What was that? she wondered. I hope it was a squirrel or a rabbit. Jesse walked on.

Under her feet she felt stones and sticks. Sometimes a vine caught at her shoes. The night sounds around her were mysterious. She couldn't tell where they came from in the dark. She used to think Old Man Camber's Woods was bad in the daytime. But, it was a hundred times scarier at night.

Jesse remembered one of the stories that the kids at school told about Old Man Camber. They said his ghost walked in the woods at night under a full moon. His ghost looked for children who trespassed on his land. When he caught them, he did something terrible to them. No one was sure *what* he did. But, whatever it was, it was terrible.

What was that? Jesse thought. She saw something white. It floated on the breeze! And it was coming toward her! The white thing made a crackling sound. It was coming closer! Suddenly, it swooped and wrapped itself around her leg.

For a second, Jesse stood frozen. She couldn't move. She opened her mouth to scream, but nothing came out. Then she saw that it was just a piece of paper, a piece of white paper blown by the wind.

Jesse breathed a sigh of relief. She took the sheet of paper from her legs. It didn't have any writing on it. She folded the paper and put it in her pocket. Mikey can use this to draw on, she thought. This is for the SAVE-A-TREE bag.

"Mikey!" Jesse looked around. "Mikey, where are you?" she called. Her voice sounded strange in the quiet night. She stopped. She thought she heard something. Jesse listened again. She walked toward the sound. It got louder and louder.

Jesse saw a little form huddled against a huge tree trunk. She ran. "Mikey!" she called. "Mikey!"

A frightened face looked up. "Jesse!" he wailed. "Oh, Jesse!" He reached his little arms up. Jesse

hugged him. Mikey cried louder. Jesse cried a little, too. But, it was dark and no one could see her tears, so it was okay. She had to be brave for Mikey. After all, she was his big sister.

"I can't find Mr. Bump," Mikey wailed. "I can't find him. It's too dark. Maybe I stepped on him." Mikey's shoulders shook as he tried to stop crying.

"You didn't step on him. We'll find him tomorrow," Jesse said. "Let's go home."

"But, I want Mr. Bump," Mikey wailed.

"We'll come back tomorrow, I promise," Jesse said. "I have a surprise for you at home. Guess what I found?"

"What?" Mikey sniffled.

"Your clown cup," Jesse said.

"My clown cup? Can I drink out of it?" Mikey asked happily.

"Sure," said Jesse. "That smily clown face is waiting for you at home. Let's go."

Jesse took Mikey's hand. She led him through the trees. The leaves crunched under their feet.

"It's scary in here," Mikey said, looking around. "Are there ghosts and boogies in here?"

"Of course not," Jesse said. "There's no such thing as ghosts. Daddy said so. That's just something you believe when you're little." Jesse gently squeezed Mikey's hand. "I don't believe in ghosts because I'm eleven. That's too old to believe in ghosts." Jesse wanted to be brave for her little brother.

"How about boogies?" Mikey asked. "Do you believe in boogies?"

"No," said Jesse. "When you're eleven you won't

believe in boogies, either."

"I think I saw one," Mikey said. "I think I saw one over there." He pointed into the darkness.

Jesse didn't look. "There's no such thing as ghosts and boogies," she said.

She held Mikey's hand and walked slowly so that he could keep up. The moon's silver light showed a path through the trees. Jesse led Mikey down the path until they came out on the road. Mikey held her hand and trustingly followed.

"Here we are," Jesse said. She knelt down in the road and looked into Mikey's big brown eyes. "Are you okay?" she asked.

"I wanna go home," Mikey whined. "I'm tired."

"Well, that's where we're going," Jesse said. "Home." She stood up and took Mikey's hand again. They began walking with the moon in the dark sky behind them. A barking dog could be heard in the distance.

Mikey stopped. He tugged on Jesse's hand. "A dog," he said. "A mean dog. It's going to get us."

"Come on," Jesse said. "It's only a dog. It can't hurt us while I'm here. I'm not afraid. Come on."

They began walking again. At last they came to their own front yard. The car was parked in the driveway. All the house lights were on.

"Where have you been, young lady?" Jesse's dad's voice came from the porch. He opened the front door and called inside, "Honey, they're home!"

"Mikey? Jesse? Are you all right?" Jesse's mom ran to them. She hugged them both together.

Mikey let go of Jesse's hand. He wrapped his arms around his mother's neck. "I'm home," he said. "I didn't find Mr. Bump."

"Mr. Bump is safe and sound," Jesse's dad said. "He was in the backyard. He didn't get too far."

"Can I see him?" Mikey asked. "Can I?"

"Not right now, young man," Jesse's mom said. "Mr. Bump is in his bed. You should be in yours. You can see Mr. Bump tomorrow."

The Andrews family went into the house. "Anyone for a glass of milk before bed?" Jesse's mother asked.

"Me! Me! Me!" Jesse and Mikey shouted together.

"I want my clown cup," Mikey said excitedly. "Where is it?" He ran to the kitchen.

Jesse followed him. She took the tape off of the cup and handed it to Mikey. Jesse's parents looked at her, curiously.

"How did that get here? Where was it?" her mother asked.

"I broke it," Jesse said. "I'm sorry." It wasn't so

hard to confess, after the dogs and Old Man Camber's Woods.

"How did you fix it?" her dad asked.

"Good old Super Glue," Jesse said. Her parents grinned at her.

"Where did you find Mikey?" Jesse's mother asked.

"Old Man Camber's Woods," Jesse said. "That's where Mr. Bump's home used to be. I thought Mikey might go there."

"Good thinking," said Jesse's father.

"That's my girl," said her mother.

"We were in the woods," Mikey said. "And it was dark. There were ghosts and boogies and dogs and giants and witches and spiders and Jesse fought them all. She beat them up, too." Mikey drank from his clown cup. The milk left a white circle around his mouth.

"Wow, it sounds like you were a very brave girl tonight," Jesse's mother said. She winked at Jesse. "Dogs? Ghosts? Where did you get the courage? How did you do it?" she asked.

Jesse thought for a minute. "Well," she said. "Now that I'm almost twelve I have responsibilities." She looked over at Mikey. His brown eyes were half closed in sleep. His head nodded as he tried to stay

awake. He even looked happy.

"And he's my little brother," she said. "He's my brother and I love him, even if he is a creep." Jesse's parents smiled at her. Jesse smiled back. She knew in her heart that everything was going to be okay.